Doggie Data

Siberian Huskies

CHRISTA C. HOGAN

Black Rabbit Books

Bolt is published by Black Rabbit Books
P.O. Box 3263, Mankato, Minnesota, 56002.
www.blackrabbitbooks.com
Copyright © 2019 Black Rabbit Books

Marysa Storm, editor; Catherine Cates, interior designer; Grant Gould, cover designer; Omay Ayres, photo researcher

All rights reserved. No part of this book may be reproduced, stored in a retrieval system or transmitted in any form or by any means, electronic, mechanical, photocopying, recording, or otherwise, without written permission from the publisher.

Library of Congress Cataloging-in-Publication Data
Names: Hogan, Christa C., author.
Title: Siberian huskies / by Christa C. Hogan.
Description: Mankato, Minnesota : Black Rabbit Books, [2019] | Series: Bolt. Doggie data | Audience: Ages 9-12. | Audience: Grades 4 to 6. | Includes bibliographical references and index.
Identifiers: LCCN 2017016405 (print) | LCCN 2017032227 (ebook) | ISBN 9781680725216 (ebook) | ISBN 9781680724059 (library binding) | ISBN 9781680726992 (paperback)
Subjects: LCSH: Siberian husky–Juvenile literature. | Working dogs–Juvenile literature. | Dog breeds–Juvenile literature.
Classification: LCC SF429.S65 (ebook) | LCC SF429.S65 H64 2019 (print) | DDC 636.73-dc23
LC record available at https://lccn.loc.gov/2017016405

Printed in China. 3/18

Image Credits

Science Source: John & Maria Kapri-elian, 18; Shutterstock: Africa Studio, 8–9; Alena Stalmashonak, 10 (bttm); Alexey Savchuk, 10 (top); Dan Kosmayer, Cover (dog); Dora Zett, 18–19; Eric Isselee, 16; Four Oaks, 28; Frenzel, 14 (top); gillmar, 21 (senior, adult); HelgaMariah, 17 (rottie); Javier Brosch, Cover (doghouse); Mikeput, 24–25; Mindscape studio, 14 (bttm); Nataliya Sdobnikova, 17 (husky); Olga_i, 17 (full pg); Pressmaster, 23 (bttm); prochasson frederic, 12–13; Seregraff, 3; Sergey Bessudov, 20 (puppy); Sirko Hartmann, 4–5, 6; Svetlana Valoueva, 21 (adolescent); SVPhilon, Back Cover, 1; USBFCO, 17 (retriever); Vivienstock, 21 (middle), 31; Volodymyr Burdiak, 32; Yulia Yudaeva, 6–7; Yuriy Koronovskiy, 20 (top), 27
Every effort has been made to contact copyright holders for material reproduced in this book. Any omissions will be rectified in subsequent printings if notice is given to the publisher.

Contents

CHAPTER 1
Meet the
Siberian Husky..........4

CHAPTER 2
A Special Personality....11

CHAPTER 3
Siberian Huskies'
Features................16

CHAPTER 4
Caring for
Siberian Huskies........22

Other Resources...........30

CHAPTER 1

Meet the

Two Siberian huskies stand at the head of a sled team. The strong dogs look like wolves. They wait eagerly for a **command**. Suddenly, the sled's driver gives an order.

"Mush!"

The huskies leap forward. The other dogs follow. The snow is deep. But that doesn't stop the dogs. Instead, they power through the snow.

Smart, Hard-Working Dogs

Huskies are strong working dogs. People breed them to do jobs, such as pulling sleds. These fluffy dogs can make good pets. But they need to stay busy. Bored huskies can get into a lot of trouble.

How Big Is a Siberian Husky?

HEIGHT
at shoulder
20 TO 23.5 INCHES
(51 to 60 centimeters)

PARTS OF A SIBERIAN HUSKY

MULTICOLORED EYES

FLUFFY TAIL

STRONG LEGS

Siberian huskies were the 12th most popular breed in the United States in 2016.

CHAPTER 2

A Special

Siberian huskies are excellent with families. They love children and enjoy playing with other dogs. These friendly dogs even love strangers. They will welcome anyone into their owners' homes. But owners should be careful when introducing huskies to small animals. These dogs like to chase cats.

Sled-Pulling Dogs

Huskies were born to pull sleds. They are fast runners and have great **endurance**. They like to work hard and with a **pack**. These dogs also love the outdoors.

Huskies don't need to pull sleds to be happy. But they do need plenty of attention and time outside.

Huskies often howl when bored. Their howls can be heard from up to 10 miles (16 kilometers) away.

Husky Challenges

Siberian huskies are high-energy dogs. If bored, they will become **destructive**. They might try to run away too. These dogs are escape artists. They can climb over or dig under fences. A lot of exercise and play will keep a husky busy. A strong fence helps keep them from escaping.

Huskies are also **stubborn** dogs. Training them can be difficult. Owners must be patient and not give up.

CHAPTER 3

Siberian Huskies'

Siberian huskies are medium-sized dogs. They can weigh up to 60 pounds (27 kg). They have long, thick fur. Huskies also have tough, furry feet. They're made for walking on snow and ice.

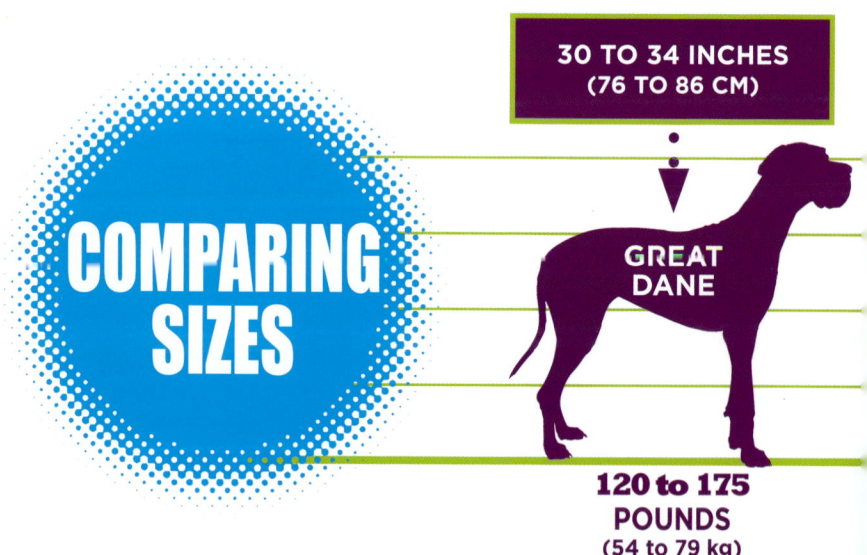

COMPARING SIZES

30 TO 34 INCHES
(76 TO 86 CM)

GREAT DANE

120 to 175 POUNDS
(54 to 79 kg)

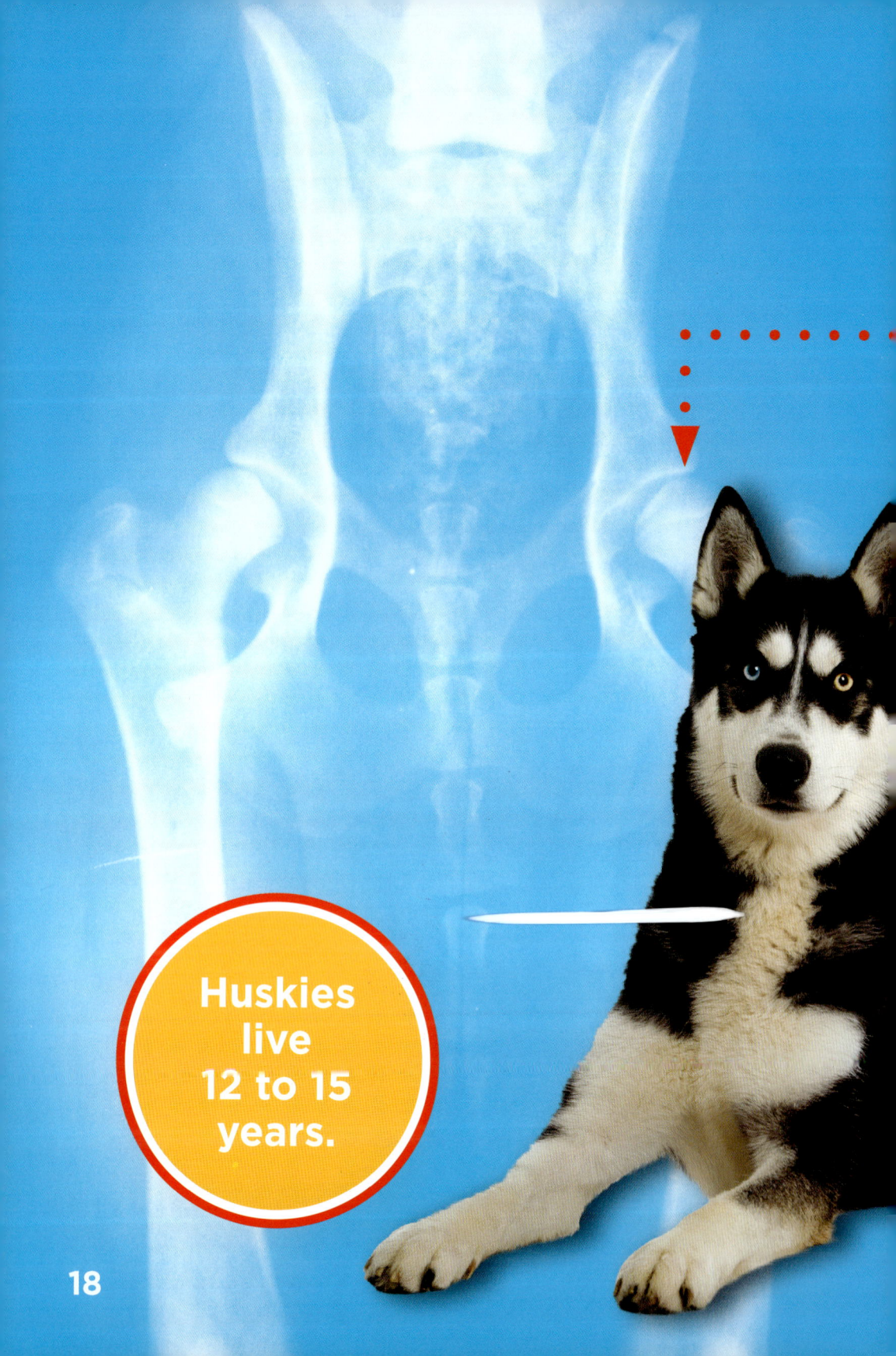

Huskies live 12 to 15 years.

Health Problems

Most huskies are healthy. However, these dogs can have hip **dysplasia**. The condition causes dogs pain when they walk.

Huskies can also get **cataracts**. Cataracts make it hard for them to see.

19

Siberian Husky Life Cycle

Pups are born with blue eyes. The color may change after five to eight weeks.

PUPPY

Senior huskies sleep more and move more slowly.

CHAPTER 4

for Siberian Huskies

Siberian huskies shed their coats twice a year. Weekly brushing keeps their fur neat. These dogs need daily brushing when shedding. Huskies also need their teeth brushed regularly. Their nails should be trimmed each month.

Grooming

brushing

nail trimming

teeth brushing

23

Eating and Exercising

Huskies need 30 to 60 minutes of exercise daily. They love to run or play. But they should avoid exercising in hot weather. Their heavy coats can cause them to **overheat**.

The amount of food huskies should eat depends on how much they exercise. Vets can help owners decide how much to feed their dogs.

Fluffy Friends

Siberian huskies make great pets for active families. They need patient owners who understand their needs. When a husky finds a good home, it becomes a pack member for life.

QUIZ

Is a Siberian Husky

Answer the questions below. Then add up your points to see if a husky is a good fit.

1 What kind of coat do you like?

A. smooth and sleek **(1 point)**

B. curly and messy **(2 points)**

C. soft and thick **(3 points)**

2 Are you a very active person?

A. Does looking for the remote count? **(1 point)**

B. I like to go out and play. But I like to relax too. **(2 points)**

C. Yes! I'm always on the move! **(3 points)**

3 How do you feel about a dog howling?

A. It's the worst! **(1 point)**

B. As long as it stops, I'm OK. **(2 points)**

C. It's fine. It's a dog's way of talking. **(3 points)**

{
3 points
A husky is not your best match.

4–8 points
You like huskies, but another breed might be better for you.

9 points
A Siberian husky would be a great buddy for your life!
}

GLOSSARY

adolescent (ad-oh-LES-uhnt)—a young person or animal that is developing into an adult

cataract (KAT-uh-rakt)—a clouding of the lens of the eye or of the transparent cover around it that blocks the passage of light

command (kuh-MAND)—an order given to a person or animal to do something

destructive (dih-STRUHK-tiv)—causing a very large amount of damage

dysplasia (dys-PLA-zhuh)—an abnormal structure

endurance (en-DOOR-uhns)—the ability to put up with strain, suffering, or hardship

overheat (o-vuhr-HET)—to become too hot

pack (PAK)—a group of animals that hunts, works, or lives together

stubborn (STUH-bern)—refusing to stop or start doing something

LEARN MORE

BOOKS
Bowman, Chris. *Siberian Huskies.* Awesome Dogs. Minneapolis: Bellwether Media, 2016.

Bozzo, Linda. *I Like Huskies!* Discover Dogs with the American Canine Association. New York: Enslow Publishing, 2017.

Johnson, Jinny. *Siberian Husky.* My Favorite Dogs. Mankato, MN: Smart Apple Media, 2015.

WEBSITES
Siberian Husky
www.animalplanet.com/tv-shows/dogs-101/videos/siberian-husky/

Siberian Husky Dog Breed Information
www.akc.org/dog-breeds/siberian-husky/

Siberian Husky Facts
www.softschools.com/facts/dogs/siberian_husky_facts/2442/

INDEX

E
eating, 25
exercising, 15, 25

F
features, 4, 7, 8–9, 12, 16

G
grooming, 22–23

H
health, 19

L
life cycles, 20–21
life spans, 18

P
personalities, 4, 7, 11, 12–13, 14, 15, 26

S
sizes, 6–7, 16–17, 21

T
training, 15, 21